Eat, Leo! Eat!

To Rita and Ingrid, for all the wonderful meals — C.A.
To Billy, my not-so-secret friend — J.B.

The Italian words in this story are

altrettanto (ahl-tret-tahn-toh): expression meaning "same to you"

babbo (BAHB-boh): dad, daddy

buon appetito (boo-ohn ap-peh-tee-toh): expression used at the start of a meal wishing others a "good appetite"

chiancaredde (kee-an-ca-rehd-deh): paving stones

chicchirichi (keek-kee-ree-KEE): cock-a-doodle-doo

creste di gallo (creh-steh dee gahl-loh): rooster's comb

delizioso (day-lee-tsee-oh-soh): delicious

farfalle (fahr-fahl-leh): butterflies

la fine (la fee-neh): the end

mangia (MAHN-jah): eat

nonna (NON-nah): grandmother

occhi di lupo (ock-kee dee loo-poh): wolf eyes

spaghetti (spah-GAYT-tee): thin strings

stelline (stel-LEE-neh): tiny stars

zia (TSEE-ah): aunt

zio (TSEE-oh): uncle

zuppa (TSOOP-pah): soup

Text © 2015 Caroline Adderson
Illustrations © 2015 Josée Bisaillon

Kids Can Press acknowledges the financial support of the Government of Ontario, through the Ontario Media Development Corporation's Ontario Book Initiative; the Ontario Arts Council; the Canada Council for the Arts; and the Government of Canada, through the CBF, for our publishing activity.

Published in Canada by
Kids Can Press Ltd.
25 Dockside Drive
Toronto, ON M5A 0B5

Published in the U.S. by
Kids Can Press Ltd.
2250 Military Road
Tonawanda, NY 14150

www.kidscanpress.com

The artwork in this book was rendered in mixed media.
The text is set in Zipty Do Std.

Edited by Yvette Ghione
Designed by Julia Naimska

This book is smyth sewn casebound.
Manufactured in Shenzhen, China, in 11/2014 by C & C Offset

CM 15 0 9 8 7 6 5 4 3 2 1

Library and Archives Canada Cataloguing in Publication

Adderson, Caroline, 1963–, author
    Eat, Leo! Eat! / written by Caroline Adderson ; illustrated by Josée Bisaillon.
ISBN 978-1-77138-013-3 (bound)
    I. Bisaillon, Josée, 1982–, illustrator II. Title.
PS8551.D3267E28 2015   jC813'.54   C2014-902894-6

Kids Can Press is a CORUS™ Entertainment company

Eat, Leo! Eat!

Written by Caroline Adderson
Illustrated by Josée Bisaillon

KIDS CAN PRESS

On Sunday afternoons everyone gathers at Nonna's house to eat — Leo and Mamma and Babbo, Zia and Zio and all the cousins. Everyone is always hungry for Nonna's big, noisy, *delizioso* lunch. Except —

"Where's Leo?" Mamma asks.
"Leo!" she calls. "Lunch!"
"No!" Leo calls back.

"Leo," Nonna says as the family sits down. "What's the matter?"

"I'm not hungry."

"Not hungry for *stelline*? Not hungry for little stars? Hmm."

Nonna ladles out the *zuppa*. Mamma passes around the bowls.

"Leo, do you know why the pasta in this *zuppa* is called *stelline*? There's a story," Nonna says.

"A story?" Leo asks.

"Once there was a little boy who went to see his nonna. He went at night. But at night the world looked so dark and different. 'I wish, I wish,' he said, 'that there was a light to see by.' Then he looked up and what did he see?"

"Stars?" Leo asks.

"Yes, *stelline*," Nonna says. "A thousand of them. Now *mangia*, Leo."

The next Sunday afternoon the whole family
gathers around Nonna's table. Almost the whole family.
"Where's my Leo?" Babbo asks.
"Leo!" he calls. "Lunchtime!"
"No!" Leo calls back.

"Leo," Nonna says. "What's the matter?"

"I'm not hungry."

"Not hungry for *chiancaredde*? Not hungry for paving stones?"

Nonna dishes out the pasta. Babbo passes around the plates.

"Do you know why this pasta is called *chiancaredde*? There's a story. Do you want to hear it?"

"Okay," Leo says.

"Once there was a little boy who went to see his nonna. He went at night with the light of a thousand stars to guide him. But the road was rocky and his feet were bare. Every step he took hurt. 'I wish, I wish,' he said, 'that this road was paved.' Then he looked down and what did he see?"

"Paving stones?" Leo says.

Nonna nods. "*Chiancaredde*. Now *mangia*, Leo."

The next Sunday afternoon at Nonna's house,
Cousin Sandro says, "I'm starving. Where's Leo?"
"Leo!" Cousin Ella calls.
"No!" Leo calls back.

"Leo," Nonna says. "Not hungry again?
Not hungry for *occhi di lupo*? For wolf eyes?"
    Nonna dishes out the pasta. Zio passes around
the plates.
    "Why is it called *occhi di lupo*?" Leo asks.
Nonna only smiles.
    "Please tell me!" Leo says, and everyone laughs.
    "He's hungry for stories," Babbo jokes.

"Once there was a little boy who went to see his nonna. He went at night by the light of a thousand stars, along a path of paving stones. After he had been walking for a while, he realized he was being followed. 'I wish, I wish,' he said, 'that when I look behind me, I won't see anything.' Then he looked and what do you think he saw?"

"Oh, no!" Leo says.

Nonna nods. "*Occhi di lupo.* Wolf eyes."

"Ah-ooooooo!" Cousin Sandro howls.

"Now *mangia*, Leo," Nonna says.

"But what happened to the boy?"

"She'll tell you next week, Leo!" everyone calls.

The next Sunday afternoon at Nonna's house,
Zia asks, "Where's that Leo?"
   "Leo!" she calls. "We're ready to eat!"
   "No!" Leo calls back.

Leo sees what's on Nonna's table. "Spaghetti? I love spaghetti!"

"I know," Nonna says.

"Now tell me about the boy," Leo says. "Please."

Nonna dishes out the pasta. Zia passes around the plates.

"Once there was a little boy who went to see his nonna. He went at night by the light of a thousand stars, along a path of paving stones, when all the wolves were out."

"Ah-ooooooo!" everyone howls.

"The boy was terrified. 'I wish, I wish,' he said, 'that there wasn't a wolf behind me!'"

"But there was!" Leo says.

"That's right. But then the boy remembered what was in his pocket. What do you think was there?"

"Spaghetti?" Leo asks.

"That's right! String. The boy quickly tied the string to a tree. He stretched it across the road. The wolf came along, and when he tripped on the string, the boy tied him up."

"Now mangia, Leo," everyone calls.

The next Sunday afternoon —
surprise! Leo is the first at Nonna's table.
"Leo!" she says. "What would you like
for lunch?"
"The rest of the story, please."
He calls, "Come on, everybody!
It's time for lunch!"

Mamma and Babbo, Zia and Zio and
all the cousins sit down. Nonna carries
in a platter. "How about *creste di gallo*?"
"With the story," Leo says. He passes
around the plates.

"Once there was a little boy who went to see his nonna. He went at night, by the light of a thousand stars, along a path of paving stones, where wolves prowled. All night he walked, so frightened. He caught a wolf and tied it up. 'I wish, I wish,' he said, 'that morning would come.' Then he heard a sound. What do you think it was?"

"What?" everyone asks.

"*Chicchirichi! Cock-a-doodle-doo!*"

"Morning!" Leo says.

"*Chicchirichi! Chicchirichi! Chicchirichi!*" everyone calls.

"That's right. And here's the *creste di gallo*, the rooster's comb." Nonna sets down Leo's plate.

"Did the boy reach his nonna's house?"

"I'll tell you next time. Now *mangia*, Leo. *Mangia.*"

And the next Sunday Leo and Mamma and Babbo come
early to Nonna's so Leo can help with her big, noisy, *delizioso*
lunch. Leo turns the crank on the pasta maker. Sheets of
dough unroll into Nonna's waiting hands. She cuts the sheets
into little squares. Then Leo pinches them in the middle.

"Please tell me the rest of the story," Leo says.

"When we eat," Nonna says.

Soon everyone arrives and gathers around the table.
Nonna carries in the platter.

"The story, Nonna!" everyone calls out. "The story!"

"Once there was a little boy who went to see his nonna. He went at night by the light of a thousand stars, along a path of paving stones, where wolves prowled. All night he walked. In the morning he arrived just as the rooster was crowing and the sun was starting to warm the world. 'I wish, I wish,' he said, 'that Nonna will be waiting for me.' Then he saw something in her garden, something like a cloud, but full of color. What do you think it was?"

"What?" Leo asks.

"*Farfalle!*" everyone calls out.
Nonna nods and laughs.
"Butterflies. A thousand of them
surrounding him and Nonna, their
arms around each other, holding
tight."

And Leo says, "The end!"

"Yes, *la fine!*"

Mamma and Babbo, Zia and Zio and all the cousins laugh.

"*Buon appetito!*" Leo calls to everyone.

"*Altrettanto,* Leo! You, too!"

A bit about pasta

Pasta is one of Italy's most famous foods. It comes in many forms — long, short, stuffed, miniature, dumpling-like and *strascinati* (strah-shee-nah-tee), shaped by hand. While the dough is usually made from wheat flour and water, it can also contain eggs; milk; flours of corn, chestnut, bran or barley; breadcrumbs; or vegetables such as potatoes, spinach, beets and even nettles. The variety of fillings is vast. Every region has its own pasta specialties, and many have names inspired by their shapes. Here are some:

Orecchiette [oh-rehck-kee-eht-teh]: little ears

Candele [kahn-day-leh]: candles

Campanelle [kahm-pah-nell-leh]: little bells

Denti di cavallo [den-tee dee kah-vahl-loh]: horse's teeth

Bardele [bahr-dell-eh]: ribbons

Anelli [ah-nell-lee]: rings

Lumache [loo-mah-keh]: snails

Gigli [jeel-yee]: lilies

Vermicelli [vehr-mee-chell-lee]: little worms

Cappelletti [kahp-pell-let-tee]: little hats

Conchiglie [kong-keel-yeh]: shells

Gemelli [jay-mell-lee]: twins

Manicotti [mah-nee-kot-tee]: sleeves

Margherite [mahr-gay-ree-teh]: daisies

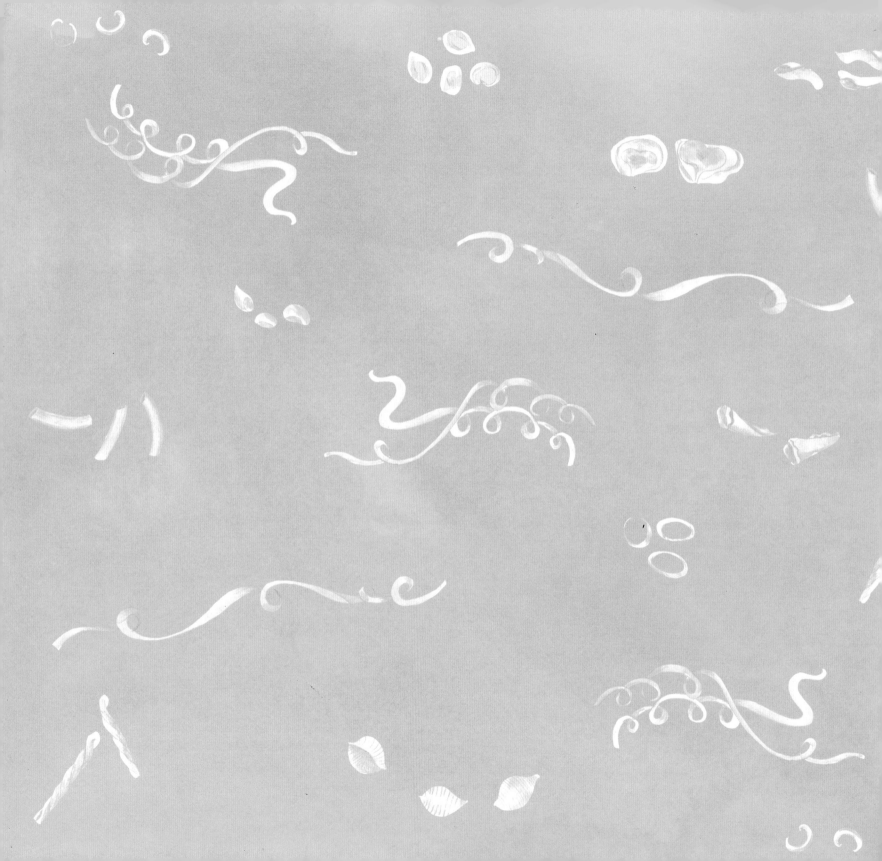